BIONICLE®

RAHI BEASTS

*FIND THE POWER,
LIVE THE LEGEND*

The legend comes alive in these exciting BIONICLE® books:

BIONICLE

RAHI BEASTS

BY GREG FARSHTEY AND JEFF JAMES

SCHOLASTIC INC.

New York   Toronto   London   Auckland   Sydney
Mexico City   New Delhi   Hong Kong   Buenos Aires

To Dawn, Chris, Patrick, and Kyle, for their love and mudgets.
To Greg, for his humor and friendship. —Jeff

For my favorite Rahi—Freddie, Sweetums,
Mr. Kitty, and Gem. —Greg

ISBN 0-439-69622-4

12 11 10 9 8 7 6 5 4 3 2   5 6 7 8 9 10/0

Printed in the U.S.A.
First printing, June 2005

BIONICLE

RAHI BEASTS

LEGO® Magazine announced a new contest in early 2003. Readers were invited to build their own Rahi beast and send in a photo of it, along with a brief description of their creature, for the chance to win **BIONICLE**® sets and the chance to see their creature in a **BIONICLE** comic.

The response was overwhelming. More than 5,000 entries poured in, including some amazingly creative models. It was so exciting to see what the fans came up with that we asked the publishers of this book to include the grand prize winner and some of the very best of the other winning entries. You've already seen one — the Tahtorak on the cover — and you'll find more in these pages.

Thanks to all the fans who helped to create this book and who make the **BIONICLE** world so much fun to work on!

Greg Farshtey & Jeff James

I am Rahaga Norik. I have been asked by my partners to write a brief introduction to our guide to the Rahi beasts of Metru Nui. As I carve these words into stone, many of the creatures in this book are loose in the city of legends. A massive earthquake shattered the Onu-Metru Archives, setting them free to stalk the night.

The Rahi discovered that the city was now a more dangerous place. Hordes of Visorak, spiderlike creatures from another land, have invaded Metru Nui. They hunt anything that lives, wrapping Rahi up in web cocoons and often using venom to mutate the Rahi into even more monstrous beings.

In the many, many years since we became Rahaga, my friends — Gaaki, Pouks, Bomonga, Iruini, and Kualus — have joined with me to dedicate our lives to protecting wild creatures from the Visorak. It has been both a difficult and dangerous task, but one vitally important to the future of our world.

If we succeed, then those who read these words will know better how to live with these creatures. If we fail, this may be the only record that these creatures ever existed.

WHAT ARE THE RAHI?

Rahi is a Matoran word that can be roughly translated to mean "wildlife." The term encompasses creatures of the land, air, and sea. Rahi come in all different sizes, shapes, and danger levels. Some are not very bright and rely solely on instinct. Others, like the Frost Beetles, are almost frighteningly intelligent. The first thing anyone who seeks to trap Rahi must know is that you cannot assume all of these creatures think and act the same.

Many Rahi are aggressive and skilled hunters. You may think you are stalking a Muaka, when in fact it is stalking you. Some Rahi hunt for food, others will attack to protect their territory, and a few species consider every other living thing to be their enemy.

Respect the power of Rahi. Understand that the smallest creature may be the most dangerous, while the largest may simply wish to be left alone. If your goal is simply to avoid being attacked, use common sense. Stay away from Rahi nests and lairs, do not attempt to frighten or harm them in any way, and most of all, be aware of what sort of creatures may be in the area. A wanderer in Ko-Metru will face far different threats than one in Po-Metru. Be prepared!

THE HISTORY OF THE RAHI

Little is truly known about the origins of Rahi, where they first appeared, or why. It appears that the first Rahi may have been ancient sea creatures of tremendous size. Some of these specimens made their way to the ocean surrounding Metru Nui years ago. They were captured and placed in the Archives for research purposes. Later, when the project was about to be cancelled, an Onu-Matoran named Mavrah smuggled the creatures out of the city. It was later learned that he had taken them to a tunnel network between Metru Nui and the island above, where they were living in relative peace.

That tranquility would be shattered by the arrival of the Toa Metru, who were journeying by water to find a new home for the Matoran. Suspecting they were there to harm the creatures, Mavrah ordered the Rahi to attack them. The Matoran realized his mistake in the end, but apparently perished when he was swept into the water during the battle. The fate of the creatures is unknown.

The city of Metru Nui was never intended to accommodate large numbers of Rahi. Indeed, there were virtually no creatures present at its founding. Over time, however, more and more wild things began to make appearances there. It was later theorized that they were driven from their homelands by the Visorak and fled by air, sea, and through long-abandoned chutes to Metru Nui.

Their arrival posed a huge problem for the Matoran, who were unprepared for the sudden onslaught of fierce Rahi. They first responded by building Kralhi, and later Vahki, to protect the city and its inhabitants. Meanwhile, Onu-Matoran began construction of the Archives as a place to hold captured Rahi.

A procedure was soon in place: Rahi who were deemed a threat to the population, along with at least one specimen of every species, were captured by the Vahki. They were then placed in stasis tubes in the Archives, which kept them alive but in suspended animation. There, the Matoran were able to monitor the Rahi and the archivists could study them. Any Rahi too large for the stasis tubes were locked up in the sub-levels.

It was not a perfect system. Some Rahi were known to escape from the tubes, while others made homes in the lowest levels or in the maintenance tunnels. It rapidly became too dangerous for even Vahki to go into some of those places, so they became wild areas.

Not all Rahi were considered to be dangerous menaces, of course. Some, like Ussal Crabs, were tamed and put to use in Matoran society. Others were considered to be harmless, or at worst, pests. It seemed that a balance had been struck between Matoran and the wildlife in their city.

It wouldn't last.

RAHI TODAY

A strange double eclipse that struck Metru Nui and an ensuing earthquake signaled a new chapter in the story of Rahi. Hundreds of stasis tubes were cracked open by tremors, freeing their contents. Predators and prey escaped from the Archives, only to find the city above largely in ruins. Frightened, hungry, and hunted by Visorak, Rahi have made this new city of shadows an even more dangerous place.

DOMAIN: ONU-METRU

These small Rahi originally dwelled in **Po-Metru**, but when the number of assemblers' villages increased, they were forced to migrate. The majority wound up in the Archives, living in shadowy corners of the vast museum and feeding on insects and microscopic protodites.

Of all Rahi, Archives Moles are probably among the best at working together. Since they are small and relatively defenseless against large predators, cooperation is the only thing that allows them to survive. They have been known to form living ladders to reach high places and living bridges to cross chasms beneath the sub-levels.

The Archives Moles' approach to dealing with the Visorak is simple: run and hide. They can squeeze into spaces far too narrow for a Visorak and can remain there, frozen with fright, until the spider creature gets frustrated and leaves. Unfortunately, the Visorak sometimes spin webs and block the openings of those spaces, trapping the moles inside. Rahaga Bomonga always keeps an eye out for anything that looks like stray webbing down below, as it often marks an Archives Mole hiding spot.

Rahaga Bomonga says: "Even the small, harmless creatures are stalked by the Visorak. I do what I can to save them, but it is not easy to coax them from their places of refuge. They are afraid . . . and with good reason."

DESIGNED BY MATTHEW NICHOLS

DOMAIN: LE-METRU

The Artakha Bull is one of the oldest Rahi known to the Matoran, with Archives records dating back well over two thousand years. It is believed to be the inspiration for the legend of the mutant Kane-Ra who guards a tunnel network. Other tales say the Artakha Bull was actually present on Metru Nui before Matoran civilization arose.

It is this latter story that led to these Rahi being named after Artakha, the legendary Matoran place of refuge. According to the tales, these creatures have intelligence far beyond Matoran level. As a result, they were the only creatures allowed by Mata Nui to share Artakha with the Matoran.

Most of this, of course, is probably myth. What is known about the Artakha Bull is that it is swift, strong, an excellent tracker, and seems to be generally hostile. If they were good-natured creatures at any point in the distant past, they certainly are not now.

Rahaga Bomonga says: "It's a smart creature. Catching it means you have to be even smarter. The fact that so many are still running around loose in Metru Nui tells you I'm not smarter . . . yet."

DESIGNED BY BRYAN CHOW

DOMAIN: ONU-METRU

One of the most powerful Rahi known to be in the Onu-Metru Archives sub-levels, the Blade Burrower has been a menace to Matoran for years. Using its powerful claws, it can dig tunnels that closely resemble Matoran made ones. Archivists have been known to mistake these passages for parts of the Archives, wander down them, and never be seen again.

Blade Burrowers hunt largely by smell, having very poor eyesight. When food is scarce in the sub-levels, they have been known to venture up to the public levels, causing huge amounts of destruction. Vahki order enforcement squads have in the past been hard-pressed to contain an enraged Blade Burrower, which often uses its long, clublike tail as a flail to knock down and disperse its enemies.

Thankfully, Blade Burrowers seem to be few in number. Visorak patrols have made efforts to capture them, so far with limited success.

Rahaga Bomonga says: "When I lived in the Archives, I tried mapping the Blade Burrower tunnels. They don't seem to be random at all. It seems like they are building something. What it might be, and why, I don't know."

DESIGNED BY DANIEL SETTLE

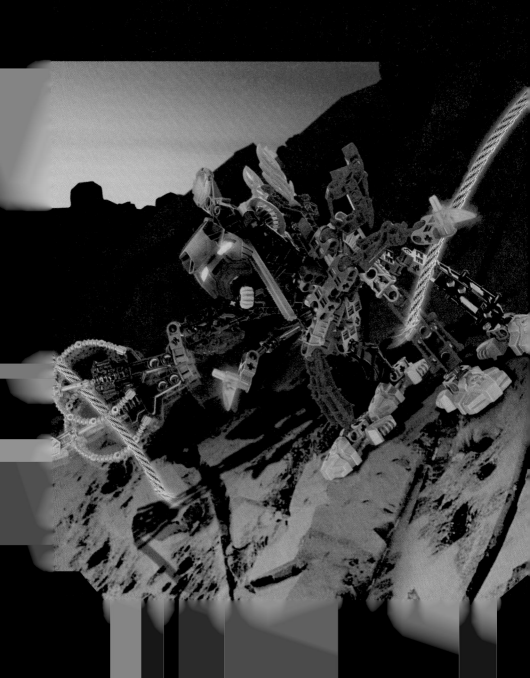

DOMAIN: ONU-METRU

The tangle of chutes, cables, and other structures are
a popular home for Rahi of many types, including the
enigmatic Cable Crawler. This bizarre creature makes its
home in the cables that overhang Le-Metru, preying upon
other climbing Rahi and small birds.

Although generally shy and reclusive around Matoran, the
Cable Crawler has been a particularly bothersome pest.
Lurking in the upper reaches of Le-Metru, this Rahi has a
tendency to use its two sharp claws to slice through power
cables and other important structures while looking for
prey. Cable Crawlers can see in the dark and prefer to hunt
by night. One of the most intriguing aspects of this creature
is its ability to unleash blasts of energy that can upset the
balance of its enemies, and can often cause vertigo. This
attack allows it to quickly overcome smaller prey and to
disorient larger enemies, giving the Cable Crawler time
to flee.

Cable Crawlers have been known to nest inside the cargo
holds of Matoran airships. This was not discovered until a
shipment of Rahi bound by air for the Archives was found
devoured when the hold was opened. The Crawlers had
taken advantage of the helpless creatures and made short
work of the lot.

Rahaga Iruini says: "Hard to spot and hard to capture. They
know the cables well and can disappear into them in an
instant. Although climbers are my specialty, Bomonga has
been a great help in catching these with his ability to stay
completely still for hours at a time and lure them close.
Total surprise is the only way to snare a Cable Crawler."

DOMAIN: PO-METRU

For sheer savagery, the Catapult Scorpion knows few equals. From their nests in the caverns beneath the Sculpture Fields, these insectlike creatures emerge on rare occasions, leaving utter devastation in their wake. Phase Dragons, Rock Raptors, Tunnelers, and Po-Matoran alike know to stay as far away as possible when these Rahi are on the surface.

At first glance, a Catapult Scorpion might be mistaken for a large Nui-Jaga. This is a common and often fatal mistake, for this Rahi is far more hostile and dangerous. With its two razorlike pincers, sharp teeth, and a head covered with spines and horns, it is already a fearsome creature. But its appearance is just the tip of the statue, as they say in Po-Metru.

This scorpion's most effective tool is its "catapult" stinger. In some manner never explained, the Catapult Scorpion is able to materialize a ball of molten magma at the end of its tail, which then quickly hardens into solid rock. The scorpion then snaps its stinger forward, sending the projectile at its foes. Unfortunately, a Catapult Scorpion considers almost anything that moves its enemy, except for Kikanalo. This makes it a very disruptive visitor to the surface world.

Rahaga Norik says: "If you are looking for a Catapult Scorpion — and I can't imagine why you would want to do that — look for Kikanalo. These Rahi eat solid protodermis, and their preferred hunting method is to follow along behind Kikanalo herds and consume whatever the beasts' horns dig up. With the herds on the wane, Catapult Scorpions have been forced to wander out of Po-Metru in search of food."

DESIGNED BY CODY FULLMER

DOMAIN: CITY-WIDE

One of the most dangerous creatures in Metru Nui, Chute
Lurkers are fortunately quite rare. They are omnivorous, but
what makes them distinct is their preferred hunting grounds:
the interior of Metru Nui chutes. These creatures are capable
of breathing liquid protodermis, and although they can
breathe air just as well, they avoid being outside of chutes
any more than they have to be.

Chute Lurkers hunt by locking themselves in place inside a
chute with their arms, then waiting for objects, other Rahi,
and even Matoran to come speeding toward them. Once
something is caught by a Chute Lurker, there is rarely any
escape unless aided by another Matoran or a Vahki. Chute
Lurkers tend to wait near sharp curves and other areas
where a traveler is less likely to spot them ahead of time.

With much of the chute system damaged by the Great
Cataclysm, Chute Lurkers have had to find other hunting
grounds. Emerging from the chutes has made them targets
for the Visorak, and there is no telling what the future holds
for the species.

Rahaga Norik says: "I have run into my share of these
creatures. Deprived of their usual hunting method, they
seem lost and confused. It's only a matter of time before
hunger makes them desperate, and desperate Rahi make
mistakes. That is something no Rahi can afford in a city
ruled by Visorak."

DOMAIN: THE COLISEUM

These generally harmless creatures play an important role in the Visorak world. The various species of Visorak feed off the energy of the Colony Drone Rhotuka spinners, making them essential to the survival of the horde. The Visorak bring large groups of drones with them when they travel to a new land, keeping the drones captive until the Visorak need them.

If the Colony Drones object to their treatment, they have not shown any signs of distress. It may be that they simply aren't smart enough to realize how they are being used. It's also possible they have been intimidated by the Visorak for so long that they simply know no other way of life.

Rahaga Iruini and Bomonga have both suggested that the Rahaga should unleash Metru Mantis on the Colony Drone pens, wrecking the enclosures and setting the drones free. This would go a long way toward crippling the operations of the hordes. Norik and Gaaki have refused to go along with the plan, pointing out that the drones would probably be hunted down and wiped out by other Rahi. Dooming a species to extinction is seen as too high a price to pay even to stop the Visorak.

Rahaga Norik says: "There has to be another way. I refuse to believe the only way we can beat the Visorak is to behave like them. The drones are not responsible for all this. They should not have to suffer for it."

DOMAIN: KO-METRU

High atop the cold crystal towers of Ko-Metru, these Rahi
can be seen scurrying from one icy rooftop to the next. The
Crystal Climber has sharp claws to hold tight onto cold
and slippery surfaces and a long, thin tail it uses for balance.
Possessing excellent night vision, their glowing red eyes are a
common sight in the evening darkness in Ko-Metru.

The Crystal Climber's favorite prey are the Ice Bats that
nest high in the Knowledge Towers. Given that the bats have
always been regarded as pests, one would think Ko-Matoran
would have welcomed the Crystal Climbers' activities. But
once these Rahi find what seems to be a good hunting area,
they are almost impossible to get rid of. Entire Knowledge
Tower chambers have had to be closed temporarily while
Vahki try to root the climbers out. Now that there are so
few Vahki left, these bestial Rahi have made the Knowledge
Towers their permanent home.

Crystal Climbers form small, tight-knit groups and react
violently to intrusions by others of their species. Ko-Matoran
have theorized that this is because too many Crystal
Climbers in one spot can cause portions of Knowledge
Towers to collapse, so they have learned not to congregate in
large numbers.

Rahaga Iruini says: "Ko-Metru is no place to climb. Slip and
fall to your doom, sure, but not climb. The trick to catching
Crystal Climbers is getting to them, since they favor the very
highest points in a Knowledge Tower. Then, once you have
them snagged with a spinner, make sure they don't fall off
the tower — they make a heck of a mess down below."

DESIGNED BY JONATHAN MASTRON

DOMAIN: GA-METRU

Commonly seen in the lakes and canals of the Ga-Metru district, the docile Dermis Turtle is particularly fond of unrefined liquid protodermis pools. The hard silver shell of the Dermis Turtle is almost impervious to attack, and its sharp silver tusks can be used in defense when needed. It has traditionally been a peaceful creature, fighting only when attacked.

A Ga-Matoran named Macku first discovered the Dermis Turtles many years ago during one of her canoe expeditions. Since that time, their numbers have seemed to explode almost to the point of making them pests. Turaga Dume at one time considered banning them from the city, and it was only impassioned arguments by Macku and Nokama that changed his mind.

One of the unusual talents of these Rahi is the ability to detect upcoming changes in the weather. When these creatures retreat into their hardened shells, chances are good that a powerful storm is just a day or two away. Matoran often use the phrase "dermis shell weather" to indicate unpleasant weather conditions.

Rahaga Gaaki says: "Another unusual feature of the Dermis Turtle is its melodic cry. In some areas of Ga-Metru, residents had grown accustomed to — and in some cases, enjoyed — the 'singing' of these creatures in the night."

DESIGNED BY JONATHAN SHEPPARD

DOMAIN: GA-METRU

This multiheaded serpent is one of the most feared and hated Rahi in all of Ga-Metru. It first appeared in the city shortly after a trading boat arrived at the docks from another land. Ga-Matoran were surprised to find no one aboard the ship, though the cargo was still intact. What they did not realize as they inspected the vessel was that Doom Vipers were already slithering from their hiding places on board into the heart of the metru.

Residents rapidly discovered just how dangerous this serpent could be. A Doom Viper's breath is a toxic compound, capable of killing any plant or animal life it touches (except, of course, itself and others of its kind). Only the Vahki, being machines and thus immune to the venom, have had any success against these Rahi. Now that the order enforcers are otherwise occupied, Doom Vipers wander Ga-Metru at will. They have been captured in the past by Visorak, but even the webbing of the spider creatures weakens when exposed to the viper's venomous power.

Given the difficulty of capturing Doom Vipers, the Visorak have made efforts to contain these creatures, often herding them into enclosed spaces and then sealing them in with rock and stone. Now and then, another Rahi seeking a hiding place unearths one of these tombs, only to discover to its regret that the Doom Vipers inside are still alive. The same cannot often be said for their Rahi rescuer.

Toa Norik says: "I cannot stand by and watch something even this repulsive fall to the Visorak. Capturing a Doom Viper means keeping your distance and making sure it is unconscious before going near. Bomonga discovered a few stasis tubes still intact in the Archives, so I am keeping these monsters stored in them, where I hope they will stay forever."

DESIGNED BY ALLEN PROULX

DOMAIN: PO-METRU

Despite its size and sharp horns, the Fader Bull may look like a Rahi who would be easy prey for a Muaka or any other predator. But don't be fooled: this beast is one of the most difficult to capture in all of Metru Nui. Its skill at escaping traps has made it a source of constant frustration to the Visorak.

No one knows where Fader Bulls originally came from, or why they have the abilities they do. What is clear is that they apparently have a natural power similar to that of a teleportation Kanoka disk. When threatened, Fader Bulls vanish, leaving only a ghostly afterimage of themselves that slowly fades away. The bull then reappears someplace well away from the danger. How much these Rahi are able to control the distance and direction of their teleportation is not known. In the past, Po-Matoran have occasionally stumbled on a Fader Bull that had materialized inside a rock or other solid object.

Fader Bulls are plant eaters, surviving on the sparse vegetation that grows in the rocks of Po-Metru. During the Morbuzakh plant's attack on the city, the Fader Bulls helped keep some areas of the metru safe by consuming its vines. Although their sheer numbers can at times make them destructive, Po-Matoran eventually learned to accept their presence. With a Rahi that vanishes at will, what else could they do?

Rahaga Pouks says: "The trick to trapping Fader Bulls is to remember they're herd Rahi. Where one goes, the others follow. Rig up a rockslide to scare them. Then keep an eye out to see when the first fader vanishes and where it reappears. Get over to that spot and maybe you can catch the third or the fourth bull as it pops back in ... assuming it doesn't reappear on top of you."

DESIGNED BY MATTHEW LONGUA

DOMAIN: KO-METRU

Frost Beetles are a classic illustration that nothing is what it seems. On the surface, they resemble sizeable insects with a pretty hostile nature. But some believe their behavior masks an almost Matoran-level intelligence and that their habit of living near Knowledge Towers is something more than just coincidence.

Heavily armored and wielding razor-sharp claws, the Frost Beetle is more than able to defend itself against predators. It could easily drive away other small creatures and claim much of Ko-Metru for itself. Instead, this species seems to spend most of its time trying to force its way into the towers. Even more startling, Frost Beetles have been known to consume the crystals used to grow new Knowledge Towers.

Matoro once proposed a theory that some of these creatures may have eaten memory crystals and somehow absorbed the knowledge inside them, passing it on to others through a sort of hive mind and thus increasing the intelligence of the entire species. Farfetched as that might be, it would explain their behavior. They have tasted knowledge — and they want more.

Rahaga Norik says: "From what Nuju has told me, it might almost be better to let the Visorak have these creatures. With the Knowledge Towers now unguarded, there is no telling what damage they might do if they find a way inside. Whatever the truth is about these things, I have a feeling they are quite smart enough now."

DESIGNED BY DANIEL MUELLER

DOMAIN: TA-METRU

Inhabiting the dark crevices in the foundries and forges of Ta-Metru, the reclusive Furnace Salamander was rarely seen by the Matoran who lived and worked in that area of the city. These Rahi have long, powerful limbs that let them jump great distances and scamper quickly across open ground. Their sharp claws help them cling to just about any surface, even the searingly hot walls of the furnaces. The Furnace Salamander can also glide short distances, using their spiny wings and long, flexible tails to provide precise flight control.

Roughly the same size as a Toa when standing erect, these Rahi tend to move in a hunched position that belies their strength and size. Despite their fearsome appearance, these beasts are not hostile — unless provoked. Should they become angry, they band together and attack in a swarm, easily overwhelming larger foes. One Matoran who survived such an incident described their bite as feeling like "a thousand red-hot needles."

Looking back, Toa Vakama now realizes that the behavior of the Furnace Salamanders offered a clue to what was happening in Metru Nui, if only he had noticed it. Shortly after the first appearance of the Morbuzakh plant in the city, the salamanders fled from the Great Furnace in large numbers. It was later discovered that the king root of the Morbuzakh had made that site its home, driving the Rahi out. With so many of the furnaces no longer operating, the salamanders now dwell atop the molten protodermis pipes that line the metru.

Toa Norik says: "You need patience and a quiet step if you wish to approach this Rahi, and a brave heart to even think of catching one. Furnace Salamanders are never alone. They spend their entire lives in the midst of their nestmates. Capture one and the others will be after you in seconds. So decide first how badly you really want a Furnace Salamander, because you may pay dearly for trapping one."

DESIGNED BY CASEY KINSEY

DOMAIN: CITY-WIDE

All one ever sees of a Gate Guardian is a relatively small
creature, ranging from 1.5 feet to 4 feet in height. Try to
approach one though, and long before you reach it you will
be batted aside, although the guardian will never seem to
have touched you. The reason for this is that the true Gate
Guardian is roughly two to three times the size of the one
visible — it projects an image of a smaller version of itself
while keeping its true self invisible, as a trap for the unwary.

The small version mimics the actions of the larger, unseen
guardian. For example, a sudden movement of its leg mirrors
a kick by the true guardian, whose reach is longer and
whose legs are far more powerful. Enemies often exhaust
themselves trying to bring down the small guardian they
see, never knowing their true opponent is hidden from them.
Gate Guardians are followers of the Visorak, used as sentries
for sites that are important but not so vital that a Kahgarak
is required.

If the Gate Guardian's deception is not discovered, a battle
with one can be over quickly. Toa Hordika Nokama came
very close to being defeated by one of these creatures. It was
only the sharp thinking of Rahaga Gaaki that saved her.

Rahaga Gaaki says: "Although this is not a sea creature, I am
the one best suited to comment on it. Gate Guardians are
vicious little cowards, hiding behind a false front so they can
attack at will. It is bad enough the Visorak came to Metru
Nui without bringing these foul creatures with them."

GUKKO

DOMAIN: LE-METRU

A common sight in the skies over Le-Metru, the Gukko bird favors nesting in the tangled cables of this busy city section. These graceful, peaceful creatures tend to stay in small flocks as they look for wind currents and updrafts to help prolong their flying.

The Gukko is a beautiful creature, with a long, graceful body and four slender wings. It prefers to spend most of the day gliding and soaring, the better to keep an eye out for predators. Gukko birds are very swift, which has the unfortunate side effect of attracting the speed-crazed Phase Dragons even more.

Despite a seemingly docile nature, the Gukko bird has proven to be extremely difficult to tame. Many Le-Matoran have tried to ride a Gukko bird, only to find themselves thrown off in short order. Even Matau, in his days as a Matoran, tried to ride one of these creatures with no success (as a result, he claims that Gukko cannot be tamed). Ironically, it was Nuju who became the first to ride a Gukko.

Rahaga Kualus says: "You should have seen the look on Nuju's face when we took off on the backs of Gukko birds! Mark my words, if the Toa succeed in saving the Matoran and bringing them to that island they spoke of, they will be fortunate if they have Gukko along. Peaceful types they may be, but let Nui-Rama threaten their nests, and you'll see what sort of fighters they are!"

DOMAIN: CITY-WIDE

Although its name would tend to associate it with Ko-Metru, Ice Vermin can be found everywhere in Metru Nui. Though no real threat in the past, since the fall of Metru Nui they have begun attacking larger creatures in packs. Their spinners appear to have in some way absorbed energy from the quake so that they can now cause targets to literally shake themselves apart.

Ice Vermin have far more than the Visorak to worry about. Their increased presence in the city has led to clashes with Kavinika and Stone Rats, conflicts that have weakened both sides and made them easy prey for the hordes. In addition, the constant use of their spinners has caused even greater damage to the city. More than a few Ice Vermin have wound up buried under rubble caused by tremors of their own making.

Whenua has stated that capturing Ice Vermin needs to be a priority, for two reasons. First, left unchecked they will wreck Metru Nui. Second, the possibility of Ice Vermin mutated by Visorak into something even worse is too horrible to consider.

Rahaga Bomonga says: "The trick is not capturing them. The trick is keeping them from bringing down buildings while you are doing it. Still, Ice Vermin aren't hard to find, even in the dark. Just look for a quake."

DOMAIN: CITY-WIDE

Kahgarak are an extremely powerful type of Visorak spider, ranging in size from 6 feet tall and 9 feet wide to 12 feet tall and 18 feet wide. They serve as lieutenants for Roodaka and Sidorak, guarding vital spots such as the Coliseum or leading parts of the horde on hunts.

The Rhotuka spinners of the Kahgarak can cloak an opponent in a field of shadow which will move with them wherever they go. While the target can survive in the dark field, they cannot hear or see anything beyond it nor are they able to communicate with anyone outside it. To an outsider, it appears as if the Kahgarak's enemy has simply been swallowed by shadows and has disappeared.

Kahgarak also have the ability to use their spinners to open a gap in the Zone of Shadow, allowing the Zivon to emerge. Since they can also send the Zivon back, the Kahgarak are the only thing that prevents the horde from being wiped out by the Zivon's appetite. Some Kahgarak have also been fitted with projectile launchers for use in sieges.

Rahaga Pouks says: "They come in different sizes and colors, but unfortunately, all have the same personality: foul. Iruini once suggested that we target the Kahgarak after a Zivon has been summoned and make it impossible for the Visorak to get rid of the monster. We rejected the idea since the Zivon would devastate everything in sight if let loose."

DOMAIN: PO-METRU

The Kane-Ra Bull is one of the largest plant-eating Rahi in Metru Nui. Its size and strength are the primary reasons it has survived so long and in such numbers. Although a Muaka might consider a Kane-Ra a tempting meal, the Kane-Ra Bull's sharp horns make it a risky creature to challenge.

Surprisingly, the Kane-Ra Bull is not a herd animal. Unlike some beasts, it does not require others of its kind for protection. In addition, there is not enough vegetation in Po-Metru to support large herds. Kane-Ra tend to wander by themselves, or at most with one or two others of their species, feeding during the day and finding shelter in caves at night. A Matoran legend speaks of a tunnel maze guarded by a mutant Kane-Ra, but most believe that to be purely fiction.

Under normal circumstances, Kane-Ra are not a threat to Matoran. However, approaching one of these Rahi too quickly, or getting too close, will almost certainly prompt an attack. Kane-Ra are extremely territorial, as more than a few Nui-Jaga have found out to their regret.

Rahaga Pouks says: "If a Kane-Ra charges at you, don't run! Unless you're wearing a Mask of Speed, you won't outrun it. Stand perfectly still, arms at your sides, and avoid looking the Rahi right in the eyes. If it decides you're not a threat, it may break off its charge before it gores or flattens you. If it doesn't, well, you won't be around to complain about the bad advice I gave you."

DOMAIN: TA-METRU

A creature of legend, the great Kanohi Dragon is a mysterious beast that seemingly vanished from Metru Nui more than a thousand years ago. Little information on this great Rahi exists in the Archives, and what data is present is open to debate and interpretation. What is certain, however, is that this great creature was one of the most powerful Rahi ever to appear in the city of legends, possibly even rivaling the combined might of the Toa themselves.

The data fragments in the Archives describe this Rahi as a monstrous, reptilian creature that emerged from the hottest furnaces and foundries in Ta-Metru. Wreathed in fire and smoke, the Kanohi Dragon could fly, slithering like an oily snake across the sky. Hot cinders and ash often fell from the dragon as it flew, leaving behind a reminder of its great power. In battle, the Kanohi Dragon relied on its fiery breath and sharp claws. At the end of its whiplike tail sprouted two smoldering blades that it used to catch opponents by surprise.

Most noteworthy of all was this creature's glistening hide, covered in overlapping scales of the hardest protodermis. Spaced throughout this armored coat were what appeared to be Kanohi masks, permanently attached to the dragon's skin. Some researchers speculated they were real Masks of Power, while others believe they were masklike protodermis growths used to draw curious Toa to their doom.

Rahaga Pouks says: "I asked Vakama about this beast. The Kanohi Dragon has evidently not been seen for generations. According to Vakama, Toa Lhikan and ten of his comrades fought a great battle against the creature and drove it away long, long ago. More than that, he did not know, and Lhikan never cared to share more of the tale. Such silence says a lot about what an awful battle it must have been."

DESIGNED BY TYLER HERBST

DOMAIN: GA-METRU

All around the outskirts of Ga-Metru, packs of wolflike
creatures called Kavinika are on the prowl. Driven out of
Po-Metru ages ago, these beasts were adopted by the Ga-
Matoran and used as guards at low-priority facilities. But
their nature proved to be so aggressive that they would
attack innocents and even each other. Efforts to drive them
away from the schools and protodermis labs proved largely
futile, and with the Matoran gone, the Kavinika rule the
night in Ga-Metru.

A Kavinika's major tools are its claws and teeth. It is also
an adept climber, scaling buildings and hiding in the shadows
to spring on any who pass below. Unfortunately, the Visorak
have learned to use this characteristic against them. Often,
one spider creature will be sent to bait a Kavinika while
the rest of the horde remains in hiding, waiting to ambush
the Rahi.

One of the strange side notes on the Kavinika is that its
population actually seems to be increasing. One theory is
that something in one of the Ga-Metru labs is causing the
Rahi to duplicate in some mysterious manner. This gives
them some safety in numbers, but also makes Ga-Metru
an even more dangerous place to wander.

Rahaga Iruini says: "Try and grab a Kavinika off its perch
and you will be lucky not to lose one or both hands. Even
after the Visorak are dealt with, we will still have to find
some way of penning up the Kavinika and finding out how
their population is growing. Otherwise, Metru Nui will
rapidly be overrun."

DOMAIN: UNKNOWN

Even to many of the Rahaga, Keetongu is considered a myth. It is said that this Rahi comes from a powerful species that was hunted to extinction by Sidorak and the Visorak horde, until one specimen remained. That Keetongu chose to go into hibernation until the day he was needed. His resting place has never been found but is actively being sought by the Toa Hordika and Rahaga.

Keetongu is an unusually powerful Rahi. His blade claw has the power to cure any being mutated by Visorak venom. His rotating shield array absorbs any power hurled against him, channels the power through the armor, and then sends it back to Keetongu's foe through a Rhotuka spinner. Keetongu's true eyes are hidden behind a crimson orb, which serves to decoy his enemies: legend says that eye can see the good or evil in anyone he encounters. He will only grant his cure to those who are truly deserving, as it takes so much energy to reverse the damage done by Visorak venom.

Keetongu is vulnerable to the spinners of Roodaka and Sidorak, and massive amounts of Visorak venom might cause harm to him as well. Whether Keetongu will ever be found, and whether he will be willing to aid the Toa Hordika, remains to be seen.

Rahaga Pouks says: "Norik insists Keetongu exists. Iruini insists he doesn't, that it's all a myth. Me? If there's a chance of a cure for the Toa Hordika, I'll do my part to find this Rahi. After all, that's a big part of the reason we came to Metru Nui in the first place."

DOMAIN: PO-METRU

The Kikanalo is a massive herd Rahi that makes its home in the canyons of Po-Metru. Using their mighty horn, they churn up the rocky ground, dislodging bits of protodermis lost during the carvers' labors. This would be an extremely positive thing, since the Po-Matoran can reuse the scraps the Rahi find, except for the fact that the Kikanalo trample entire villages in the process.

Although long dismissed as dumb beasts, Kikanalo were discovered to be unusually intelligent by Toa Metru Nokama. She credits them with assisting the Toa in a struggle with the Vahki. Kikanalo can deal with an enemy in any number of ways. Stampeding over foes is common, as is leaping high into the air and landing on top of an opponent. If pressed, Kikanalo herds can unleash a powerful roar that can blow enemies away like grains of dust in one of Toa Matau's cyclones.

Some Kikanalo still remain on the northern plains of Po-Metru, but their numbers are decreasing as the Visorak take a stranglehold on Metru Nui. Too proud to hide, the Kikanalo have tried to challenge the spider creatures head on and, more often than not, have lost. If the Visorak are not stopped, eventually there may be none of these amazing creatures left.

Rahaga Pouks says: "I've done what I can. I wish I had Nokama's old mask so I could talk to the beasts, though I doubt they would listen. They are determined to fight for what's theirs, but the Visorak have the numbers. In another two months, three at the most, the famous stampedes of the Kikanalo may be history."

DOMAIN: CITY-WIDE

Commonly found in the vicinity of the Moto-Hub, the Kinloka has also been spotted in the neighboring Ko-Metru and Ta-Metru districts as well. Although this creature resembles an insect, it is in fact a particularly vicious form of large rodent.

A distant relative of the stone rats of Onu-Metru, this Rahi seems to be the result of an experiment to produce an animal with a more efficient digestive system. The unfortunate result was a nasty beast that is always hungry and will devour anything in its path. Kinloka normally attack in large packs and are able to devour entire structures in a matter of seconds.

One unusual feature of the Kinloka is its ability to carry Kanoka disks that it flings at its opponents. What this Rahi lacks in strength and throwing distance it more than makes up for with pinpoint accuracy. This beast has been known to carry a variety of Kanoka, but it most commonly uses disks with the weaken power to slow down opponents.

Rahaga Bomonga says: "Ugly. What is worse than looking out your window to see a swarm of chittering, ravenous Kinloka headed your way? I'll tell you — still being in your dwelling when they get there."

DOMAIN: UNKNOWN

The great Onu-Metru Archives contained many strange
and wondrous creatures, but few as bizarre as the Kraawa.
Only one has ever been seen in Metru Nui, held in the most
secure section of the Archives prior to the Great Cataclysm.
Matoran researchers were fascinated by its unusual abilities,
but never pierced the mystery surrounding the creature.

At first glance, this Rahi does not seem particularly
frightening or dangerous. With a squat body and a very
long neck, the Kraawa moves with a shuffling, lumbering
gait that looks quite comical. This Rahi has two glowing
eyes, which change color from blue to red when it is in a
stressful environment.

The Kraawa's primary means of defense seems to be the
ability to absorb any force used against it and converting
the energy of the attack into physical growth. The more it is
struck, the bigger and stronger it gets. It is unknown whether
there is any upper limit to its growth potential. The Kraawa
was a difficult captive of the Archives, frequently escaping
and wreaking havoc on the facility.

Rahaga Pouks says: "That one Kraawa is loose somewhere
in Metru Nui, and no one knows where. Maybe the Visorak
already got it, though if they did, I wouldn't wager on their
ability to keep it. Finding a way to trap it without ever
striking it has been keeping me up nights, so I am in no
rush to meet the thing."

DOMAIN: ARCHIVES MAINTENANCE TUNNELS

Krahka is an intelligent, shapeshifting Rahi who for years made her home in the tunnels beneath the Archives. She has the unique ability to change her form into that of any living being she has seen, or any combination of the living beings she has seen. In the process, she gains the powers of those she imitates, can mimic their voices perfectly, and even gains some of their knowledge. Krahka is capable of speaking and understanding Matoran, forming complex strategies, and successfully deceiving virtually anyone. Only the Rahaga have been able to pierce her disguises.

The Toa Metru first encountered this Rahi while investigating a possible flood in the Archives. Krahka almost succeeded in defeating them, only to fall when she tried to duplicate the powers of all six Toa at once. Later, she aided the Toa against the Visorak. She was last seen vanishing into the Zone of Darkness along with the Tahtorak and Zivon.

Although Krahka believed for a long time that she was the only one of her kind, Rahaga Pouks revealed to her that there were actually many more Krahka in another land. The others of her species were reportedly captured by the Visorak and are now presumed to be extinct.

Rahaga Pouks says: "Some Rahi are savage, some are peaceful, some are benevolent, and some are as close to evil as you can get in a wild thing — and Krahka is all of those, and more. There's no way to plan a trap for her, because you never know what she will look like or be able to do next. So be careful — the next Rahi you see might be her."

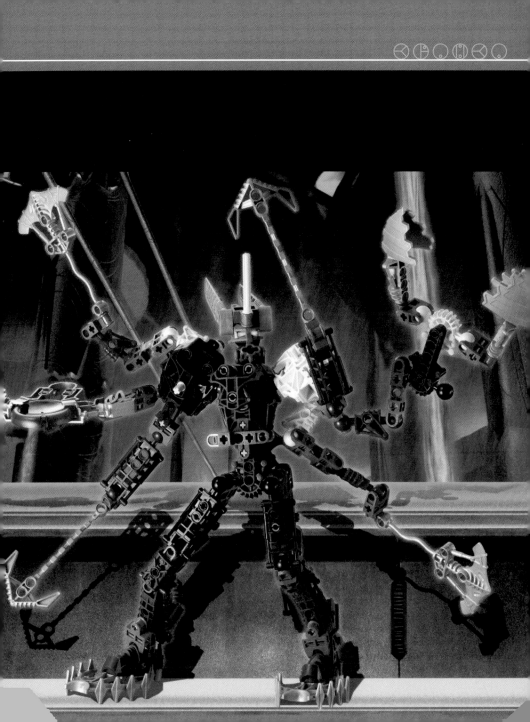

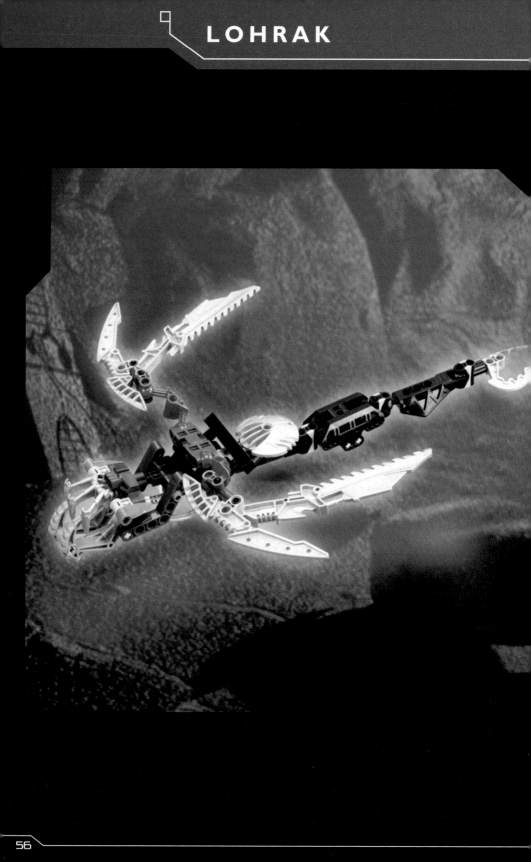

DOMAIN: CITY-WIDE

First discovered by miners in the Onu-Metru district many years ago, the Lohrak can now be found all over the city. These great, winged serpents have ragged jaws full of snapping teeth, while their scaly hides are often covered in slime and other disgusting filth. They are a terrifying sight, but their vile looks are nothing compared to their aggressive, savage behavior.

Dwellers in darkness, the Lohrak proved to be a particular problem for the archivists and maintenance workers in Onu-Metru, although every metru had Matoran who could share a frightening story of a Lohrak encounter. Workers who wandered off the job to go exploring were warned that Lohrak might lurk anywhere. For a time, the creatures were even pronounced a protected species by Turaga Dume, in hopes of stopping digging projects that might unearth more of these monsters.

The Lohrak seem to have become a "pet project" of the Visorak. The Toa Metru encountered a mutated version of one shortly after they returned to Metru Nui, and barely survived the encounter. It is possible that the hordes are planning to mutate and enslave these Rahi for use in future conquests.

Rahaga Norik says: "Normal Lohrak attack in mobs, swarming all over their prey until they bring it down by sheer weight of numbers. Mutated Lohrak are easily three to five times the size of an average specimen, and one is more than enough to create a disaster area. The best way to deal with them, short of running and hiding, is finding some way to impede their flight as they are much slower on the ground."

MANAS

DOMAIN: UNKNOWN

The Manas are strange and powerful crablike creatures whose origin and behavior remain a mystery. The only report of them came from the Toa Metru, who spotted two specimens while sailing from Metru Nui to the island above. They were dubbed "Manas," which is the Matoran word for "monster," due to their size, appearance, and savage manner.

Whenua has suggested that the Manas may in some way be related to the Ussal Crab, though Toa Matau laughs at the suggestion. Onewa's theory is that the Manas are actually creatures from Metru Nui's pre-history, who somehow survived into the present day. Nuju has stated that he does not care where they came from, only what they might do in the future.

What everyone agrees on is that they are phenomenally strong, so much so that it is doubtful that any Toa or group of Toa could defeat them unaided. Fortunately, only two have ever been spotted, and with luck no one will ever encounter them again.

Rahaga Gaaki says: "I have never seen a Manas, a fact I am very happy about. From what Nokama has told me, they are fierce, violent beasts, indeed. Imagine the destruction they would cause if they ever fell under the sway of someone truly evil!"

DOMAIN: CITY-WIDE

Although quite large — averaging six to eight feet in height — this insectlike creature does not live up to its frightening appearance. Mantis can be spotted in virtually all of the six metru, commonly staying on the outskirts and moving into the more populated areas only in search of food.

The Metru Mantis is a nocturnal meat eater, its favorite prey being Nui-Rama, Nui-Jaga, and others of its own kind. Relatively tame unless provoked, Mantis have been set free by Onu-Matoran in mines and tunnels to clear out fireflyers and other insects that might be living there. In the months since the arrival of the Visorak, the Mantis have discovered they quite like the taste of the spider creatures too. This has prompted Sidorak to assign two Kahgarak the task of hunting down and capturing every Mantis in the city.

These Rahi have never been known to attack Matoran, although they will defend themselves if threatened. Extremely fast, Mantis can catch an opponent between their strong forelegs and then bite with their mandibles. Mantis venom acts as a sedative, rapidly taking the fight out of a foe.

Rahaga Norik says: "You could call these Rahi the 'enemy of our enemy.' Knowing that the Visorak hate them, Bomonga and I have made a special effort to capture them and keep them safe in the Archives. We hope to unleash them as a strike force against the hordes at the right moment."

DESIGNED BY ERIC RICHTER

MUAKA

DOMAIN: KO-METRU

The Muaka is a powerful tigerlike beast. Nocturnal hunters, they spend days asleep in unused portions of the Archives and then emerge to prowl Ko-Metru at night. Scholars working after hours in the Knowledge Towers grew used to hearing the growls of the Muaka echoing through the district.

Muaka are solitary hunters, extremely quick for their size, and able to bring down almost any other Rahi. They are particularly fond of Rahkshi, which they consider a delicacy. A single Muaka can decimate an underground Rahkshi colony in a matter of days. Muaka do not seem to like the taste of Matoran, but the Rahi's ferocious and unpredictable temper makes it a constant danger to anyone around. Efforts to capture and train Muaka have been horrible failures.

This Rahi relies primarily on its claws when hunting. Sinking them into its prey, it forces the unfortunate victim to the ground and then finishes the job with its teeth. The Muaka will then carry its kill off to a nearby lair.

Rahaga Pouks says: "Hunting Muaka? Don't. Odds are the whole time you think you are stalking it, it is stalking you — and it's a lot better at the job. If you absolutely have to capture one, try using a Rahkshi staff or something else that has their scent on it as bait. If a Muaka is after you, make it work — running, jumping, climbing, anything. The Muaka may decide you just aren't worth all the effort and go after easier prey."

DOMAIN: CITY-WIDE

Very little is known about the Rahi flyer known as **Nivawk**. It is believed that Nivawk is its given name, not its species name. It first appeared in Metru Nui some 18 months prior to the Great Cataclysm, roughly the same time Makuta assumed the identity of Turaga Dume. Nivawk was Makuta's pet and spy, monitoring events in the city from above and then reporting back to its master.

Nivawk is an extremely powerful bird, resembling a large Rahi hawk or falcon. It is strong enough to carry a Matoran without any strain and occasionally transported "Dume" from place to place. Nivawk feeds on smaller flyers, mostly in Le-Metru, swooping down and grabbing them out of their nests. If attacked, Nivawk relies on its beak and claws for both offense and defense.

After Makuta revealed his true identity, he used a shadow claw to grab Nivawk and absorb the Rahi into his substance. Makuta later appeared with Nivawk's wings growing from his back. It remains a mystery whether this Rahi is truly dead or if there are any more of its species.

Rahaga Kualus says: "I don't even want to discuss this one, no, no. The only thing that surprised me about this foul creature was that it had the nerve to hunt living prey, rather than just scavenge among the dead. If it were still in the city, well . . . though it shames me to say it, I don't think I would try very hard to save it from the Visorak."

DOMAIN: PO-METRU

The Nui-Jaga inhabit the barren wastelands near the Po-Metru Sculpture Fields. These scorpionlike creatures are notoriously ill-tempered, quick to strike out at intruders or even each other.

Nui-Jaga commonly hunt in packs, which helps to make up for the fact that they are not very fast. One of the creatures will drive prey forward, usually into a canyon, where others wait to strike. Once the target is surrounded, the Nui-Jaga will call to each other. Their cries have been compared to the sound of glass breaking.

Nui-Jaga stings are painful, sometimes fatal. In some parts of Metru Nui, Nui-Jaga stingers are considered very valuable, so Po-Matoran have been known to hunt for the creatures. Few of the hunters ever return.

Rahaga Norik says: "You only have one advantage when trying to trap a Nui-Jaga, and that is that they are not very bright. One effective trick is to place a sheet of crystal along a path. The Nui-Jaga will see its own reflection and strike, thinking it is another of its kind. If it hits hard enough, its stinger will get buried in the rock and it can be handled easily."

DOMAIN: LE-METRU

A harsh buzz fills the air . . . a rustle of wings . . . a dark shape flying out of the sun . . . the warning signs of a Nui-Rama attack. These insectoids are one of the earliest recorded Rahi menaces in Metru Nui, and Vahki order enforcers spent centuries trying to root them all out of their Le-Metru nests.

Nui-Rama feed on liquid protodermis and Matoran believe that they are particularly attracted to the impurities in it. Drawing it directly from the ocean leaves the Nui-Rama vulnerable to sea creatures, so the insects prefer to drink their fill from the chutes. Using their stingers to pierce the magnetic field around a chute, they will drain large amounts of liquid protodermis from inside. If they return often enough to one spot, the field can be ruined and the chute collapses.

Nui-Rama use their stinger both for feeding and as an offensive tool. They are most dangerous if their nest is disturbed. A Nui-Rama's wings are strong enough to allow it to lift a Toa high in the air. The Nui-Rama's natural enemy is the Gukko bird.

Rahaga Kualus says: "Oh, my — nasty things. One of them is hard enough to deal with — anger a swarm and you will have a very short day. Best way to keep safe is to get inside immediately. If that's not possible, head for Ko-Metru. Intense cold slows the Nui-Rama down and may give you time to escape. As for capturing them, what works for the Visorak will work for you: webs, nets, anything that will entangle them."

DOMAIN: LE-METRU

Often seen racing through the tangled chutes and cables of Le-Metru, the enigmatic Phase Dragon is one of the most unusual Rahi found in the city of Metru Nui. Larger than a Toa, this creature can be frightening to look at. Sharp claws sprout from long, powerful limbs, while glistening white fangs protrude from the Phase Dragon's mouth. Flames can often be seen shooting from its maw, while dark, spiny wings help this Rahi move quickly through the skies.

Despite this terrifying appearance, the Phase Dragon has a surprisingly gentle personality. It loves speed, and has been known to chase vehicles and flying Rahi. Phase Dragons have often been spotted flying alongside Matoran airships.

The Phase Dragon also loves to race vehicles on the Le-Metru test track, where it puts its powerful phasing ability to use. Just when this Rahi is about to strike a hard surface at high speed, it changes — or "phases" — to a ghostlike consistency, allowing it to pass harmlessly through solid objects. Once the obstacle has been passed through, the Phase Dragon returns to solid form and continues racing!

Rahaga Norik says: "When the skies over Le-Metru were filled with airships and the streets with moving vehicles, the Phase Dragon was no real threat to anyone. Now that the city is largely dead, this Rahi is growing bored and has begun chasing after anything that moves. It will even charge and attack to get something to run, often misjudging its own strength and doing serious harm."

DESIGNED BY DAVID DAUT

DOMAIN: GA-METRU

These amphibious creatures dwell in the sea waters near Ga-Metru. Graceful as well as powerful, they have always been regarded with respect by the Ga-Matoran. Their great fins allow them to swim at high speeds underwater as well as more slowly through the air. Prey, normally smaller sea creatures, is grabbed using the claws on the Proto Drake's tail.

Although the ocean is liquid protodermis, that is not how the drake got its name. It actually came from the creature's strange habit of bathing in molten protodermis in Ta-Metru vats. More than one Ta-Matoran has been startled to see a violent upheaval in the fiery liquid, followed seconds later by the emergence of a Proto Drake. Onu-Matoran believe that these Rahi may attract various parasites while underwater and so use the searing hot liquid to burn them off.

Proto Drakes can be frightening, but they do not seem to be hostile to Toa or Matoran. Only once has a Proto Drake attacked Ga-Metru, and that creature later proved to be wounded and in terrible pain. Their presence has traditionally been welcomed by the residents of Ga-Metru since they primarily feed on sharks.

Rahaga Gaaki says: "Ga-Matoran must be very friendly sorts. If I saw something that size flying toward me, claws ready to grab, I don't know that I would be welcoming it with open arms. Unfortunately, the Visorak don't care if a creature is 'friendly' or not — they want them all in their web — so I will do the best I can to snare these things for their own protection."

DESIGNED BY GAR AND KEANE SECRIST

RAZOR WHALE

DOMAIN: GA-METRU

Massive creatures, Razor Whales live in the ocean off Ga-Metru, feeding on other marine life. Although their appearance is formidable, they are not by nature a hostile species. The incredibly sharp spines on their backs are enough to scare off most predators, and even Matoran fishing boats leave them in peace. Rarely having to fight, Razor Whales have found they quite enjoy living a peaceful existence.

One interesting fact about these Rahi is that at a certain point in their lives, their spines fall off. Whether that is related to age or some other factor, no one knows. But once the spines are gone, it seems to be easier to tame these beasts and some Matoran, like Macku, have even been able to ride them.

Nokama has fought hard to protect this species from the Visorak Boggarak who menace them, but it has been a losing cause. Not used to having enemies, Razor Whales do not seem to understand the need to hide or flee. The Toa Hordika keeps trying though, for each Razor Whale who is captured by the invaders is like a personal blow to her.

Rahaga Gaaki says: "Sometimes the largest creatures are the least dangerous to others. In this case, the gentle nature of the Razor Whale is working against the species. If they do not learn how to fight, they may all perish — or worse — at the claws of the Visorak."

DESIGNED BY LAWRENCE VANDERBUSH

DOMAIN: PO-METRU

Found around the Po-Metru Sculpture Fields, the Rock
Raptor is one of the main predators in this district. Although
not very aggressive towards Matoran, these Rahi are cunning
hunters with an uncanny ability to bring down prey much
larger than themselves.

They prey upon large animals like Kikanalo using a unique
method. A Rock Raptor uses its natural tools to dig out
caves in the mountains in Po-Metru as living space. It can
then use those same tools to weaken entire slopes and bring
them down in a rain of stone on Kikanalo herds or wandering
Kane-Ra. Stunned, the larger creatures are then easy prey
for the raptors.

Rock Raptors have increasingly come into conflict with
Visorak Roporak. Unfortunately for the raptors, they seem
to have met their match and their numbers are dwindling
rapidly. Worse, they are so territorial and aggressive they
will not let a Rahaga anywhere near enough to catch them,
their only hope of protection against the hordes.

Rahaga Bomonga says: "Pouks tried. Iruini tried. Even Kualus
tried to catch these things, and he hates going after anything
that doesn't have wings. Now it's my turn. If I fail, there may
soon be no Rock Raptors left to catch."

DOMAIN: GA-METRU

The Sea Spider is an amphibious creature first spotted in the ocean off Ga-Metru after the arrival of the Visorak. According to the Rahaga, the Sea Spider is a natural enemy of the Visorak and large numbers of them follow the hordes from place to place. They spend most of their time in the water, where they are safe from all of the Visorak breeds except the Boggarak.

Sea Spiders hunt by surprising their prey, then injecting venom using their forelegs. The venom physically shrinks the target to a more manageable size. The Sea Spider then uses its spinner to throw its prey into stasis until such time as the hunter is ready to feed.

Unlike the Visorak, Sea Spiders do not hunt in large groups. In fact, it seems that members of this species actively hate each other. Visorak lives have been spared in the past when one Sea Spider intervened to disrupt another's hunt. Sea Spiders have no nests or colonies or any kind of organized leadership, and will not cooperate even in life or death situations. This has limited their success against the Visorak.

Rahaga Gaaki says: "Sea Spiders are one of the only Rahi I don't try to capture, because they are a threat to the Visorak. If I did need to defeat one, I wouldn't bother to use my spinner. I would just lure a second Sea Spider to the area and let the two of them fight it out. The only thing I have ever seen a Sea Spider back away from was a Bohrok Krana in an Archives display case. No idea why that would frighten a Rahi this fierce."

DOMAIN: LE-METRU

Long before the Visorak, there was the Silver Chute Spider, one of the most voracious predators in Metru Nui. These Rahi normally clustered near transport chutes looking for prey. Incredibly strong and nearly invisible, Silver Chute Spider webbing among the Le-Metru cables was a constant hazard to Matoran workers.

The Silver Chute Spider's favorite prey was flying creatures, particularly Gukko. The birds would fly into the spider's web and become ensnared. Fast-acting venom contained in the web would then paralyze the prey. Unless a passing Matoran spotted the trouble and worked to free the bird before the spider arrived, there was no hope of escape.

Ga-Matoran researchers spent many hours studying Silver Chute Spider webs, hoping to learn how such a thin and light substance could be so strong. Had they succeeded in unlocking the secret, Matoran would have been able to create ropes and cables thinner than thread and as strong as hardened protodermis. Unfortunately, Makuta's actions ended their research.

Rahaga Norik says: "Of all the Rahi in Metru Nui, only the Silver Chute Spider seems to have escaped the notice of the Visorak. It may be that they sense some kinship to this creature. I have seen hordes sweeping through the metru, capturing every Rahi they see, yet completely ignoring these arachnids. How long that situation will last, no one knows."

DESIGNED BY DANIEL EMMONS

DOMAIN: PO-METRU

Deep in the wilds of Po-Metru, small bands of Spiny Stone Apes can be found hiding among the towering protodermis sculptures. This Rahi's mottled brown and gray hide helps it blend in easily within this rocky environment, while powerful arms and legs allow it to climb vertical surfaces quickly. Sharp climbing claws help the Spiny Stone Ape safely cross slippery surfaces, while a blade-tipped prehensile tail can be used for balance (or as an extra limb to aid in climbing).

While not especially hostile, these creatures can be very aggressive when their territory is invaded. When threatened, this beast tends to curl itself into a defensive ball, using its sharp foreclaws, bladed tail, and spiky hide to keep attackers at bay. The guttural hissing of this creature is a warning that it may attack, and Po-Matoran always know to back away slowly when hearing this noise.

The Spiny Stone Ape has a somewhat symbiotic relationship with the Rock Raptors also found in Po-Metru. While seldom found living together, the Spiny Stone Apes often use the abandoned caves and tunnels carved out of the canyon walls by the Rock Raptors. In turn, the Rock Raptors seem to tolerate this behavior, perhaps due to the Spiny Stone Apes' considerable skill in defense. A cavern guarded by Spiny Stone Apes is a secure location indeed!

Rahaga Iruini says: "The Po-Matoran were very fortunate that the Spiny Stone Ape is not overtly aggressive. This creature possesses tremendous strength, allowing it to easily lift ten times its own weight. Combine this raw power with sharp claws, a swordlike tail, and pincushion armor, and it is no wonder this Rahi has proven a threat even to Visorak."

DESIGNED BY JORDAN STEELQUIST

DOMAIN: SUBTERRANEAN TUNNELS

The largest land Rahi ever seen in Metru Nui, the Tahtorak stands 40 feet high and has enough power to wreck the city. Even more disturbing, it is apparently an intelligent creature, capable of speaking Matoran and engaging in limited conversation. Just how it learned the language is a mystery most don't find time to ponder as Tahtorak's claws and tail bring down buildings around them.

What few Archives records exist on this beast indicates it may have actually been a herd creature in some other land. It somehow ended up in the unexplored area beneath the Archives maintenance tunnels, where it was disturbed by a battle between the Toa Metru and Krahka. It later aided the Toa against the Zivon, vanishing into the Field of Shadow with its enemy at the climax of the battle. Some who have encountered the Tahtorak believe it has no idea how it got to Metru Nui and is desperate to find a way home.

The Tahtorak relies on brute strength. Its thick hide protects it from most blows, although it did prove vulnerable to the Zivon's stinger. One sweep of its tail was enough to level an entire metru block and, when idle, it would rip up sections of transport chute and see how far it could toss them. Even as an ally, the Tahtorak proved to be extremely dangerous. Much more of its "help" and there might not have been a city left to save.

Rahi Pouks says: "I am in a unique position to comment on this Rahi, since I rode on its back from Ta-Metru to Le-Metru. It's really something to feel the city shaking with each step it takes. Fortunately, I never had to try capturing it. All I can say is, I hope the beast finds its way back to where it came from, both for its own sake and for Metru Nui's."

DESIGNED BY JUSTIN LAMB

DOMAIN: GA-METRU

These lizardlike amphibians haunt the shallow water around Ga-Metru, though they have been spotted in other places along the Metru Nui coastline as well. Long a menace to Matoran navigation, Tarakava have become even more dangerous since the Great Cataclysm, as their undersea nests have been disturbed.

Tarakava usually hunt in pairs. Their preferred method is to lurk just below the water until prey comes by, then stun their victim with blows from their forelegs. Tarakava can stay under water for prolonged periods of time and are powerful enough to capsize large watercraft. They have been known to attack Matoran, but their preferred prey are larger Rahi who may come to the water to drink or any of various species of seabird.

A smart pilot whose boat is menaced by a Tarakava will head for deep water. The ocean is filled with Takea Sharks and other predators who feed on Tarakava, so these Rahi will not pursue there unless enraged or starving.

Rahaga Gaaki says: "The first thing to remember about Tarakava is that even if you can't see them, they are always there. If you are prepared for them to spring out at you, you rob them of their best tool: surprise. A Tarakava is most vulnerable when it has surfaced, lunged, and missed. That is the time to hit it with a spinner."

DOMAIN: LE-METRU

Commonly found on the shores of Ga-Metru and hauling carts in the streets of Le-Metru, the docile Ussal Crab is one of the friendliest Rahi in all of Metru Nui. No one knows for sure when the first Ussal Crabs were seen in the great city, but none can deny their importance.

The Ussal Crab seems to genuinely like Matoran company and has been easy to tame for use as a beast of burden. Their gentle personality and large numbers made the Ussal Crabs a staple of Matoran society, commonly used to carry cargo, serve as mounts, or help Matoran construction and digging crews. Onu-Matoran seem particularly fond of these creatures. They are a common sight in the Great Archives, where they help their masters move stasis tubes and other heavy objects.

Despite their somewhat ungainly appearance, Ussal Crabs can move with great, clattering speed when they wish to. This has made Ussal Crab races a popular sport among the Matoran in the city.

Rahaga Gaaki says: "This is one of the few wild creatures I have ever seen truly befriend Matoran. Orkahm spent many years with his Ussal Crab, Pewku, and now Whenua seems to have taken a liking to the Rahi. He has even gone so far as to suggest that the Toa take him with them when they leave Metru Nui for the last time."

DOMAIN: CITY-WIDE

It's rare that a Rahi gets named for what it hunts, rather than for itself. But these massive Rahi have been hailed by some and hated by others in Metru Nui for their prey of choice: the robotic order enforcers known as Vahki. In truth, though, Vahki Hunters do not just seek out those artificial creations. They have also been known to demolish Ta-Metru fire drones, industrial machinery, and anything else mechanical.

A small number of these creatures escaped from the Archives many years back and only one or two have been successfully recaptured. In the process, entire squads of Vahki have been reduced to so much scrap metal by the claws and teeth of these Rahi.

Vahki Hunters originally favored Po-Metru and Ta-Metru, but after the coming of the Morbuzakh, increased Vahki patrols made those areas too chaotic. The Rahi have now spread out all over the city, usually hiding underground. Their favorite trick is to wait for a Vahki squad to pass by overhead, then burst up through the street, grab the one in the rear, and carry it back below. It will later toss whatever parts it didn't like back onto the street.

Rahaga Kualus says: "Pouks is usually the one to hunt these, but they asked me to comment because of the wings. We can all feel lucky that Vahki Hunters stick to non-living prey. If they ever get an appetite for the rest of us, I am not sure what could stop these monsters. Certainly not the Vahki!"

DESIGNED BY NATHANIEL MACMILLAN

DOMAIN: CITY-WIDE

Hordes of these spiderlike creatures appeared in Metru Nui following the Great Cataclysm. They quickly took over the Coliseum and spread out through the metru, weaving their webs and capturing Rahi. It was later learned that many of the wild creatures who have appeared in the city over the years were in fact running away from the relentless march of the Visorak through their lands.

There are six known breeds of Visorak:

ROPORAK

Commonly used as spies for the horde, Roporak have the power to blend in with their surroundings, becoming virtually invisible. In battle, they use Rhotuka spinners with a disrupter power that drains energy from their target. Roporak are extremely cautious fighters, preferring to wait until a foe has been weakened by others before striking.

BOGGARAK

These are the only Visorak whose spinners contain two powers, which can apparently be switched back and forth by the Boggarak. When used underwater, they cause a target to swell up and float to the surface. When used on land, they remove all moisture from a target, reducing it to a pile of dust. Boggarak are also able to create a sonic hum that can transmute solid matter into gas.

OOHNORAK

Oohnorak is not a leader, but a follower, and this species is often used as a living ram when the mechanical Visorak battle rams are not available. Its spinner numbs a foe, making escape impossible. Oohnorak have limited telepathic abilities and are skilled mimics, often imitating a trusted voice to lure a foe into a trap.

KEELERAK

The most unpredictable of all six breeds, Keelerak will fight fiercely one moment, then disappear to go hunt the next. Their spinners contain an acidic venom that can eat through any substance. The ends of their legs are razor sharp, and Keelerak have been known to leap in the air and whirl at high speed, becoming Visorak "buzz saws."

SUUKORAK

Suukorak are natural tacticians, masters at knowing when to attack and when to withdraw. Their spinner creates a field of electrical energy around a target that slowly shrinks — while the field is in effect, the target cannot escape it. Suukorak also have the ability to slow their life processes down to almost zero, making it extremely difficult for others to detect their presence.

VOHTARAK

Although not gifted with the power of fire, Vohtarak spinners can create an extremely painful burning sensation in a target, so bad it cannot concentrate on anything but its suffering. Always aggressive, Vohtarak are capable of making berserker charges during which their outer shell becomes almost completely invulnerable to harm.

Rahaga Norik says: "Nothing. There is nothing to say. Look around you, you can see what they have done here . . . and why the hordes have to be crushed."

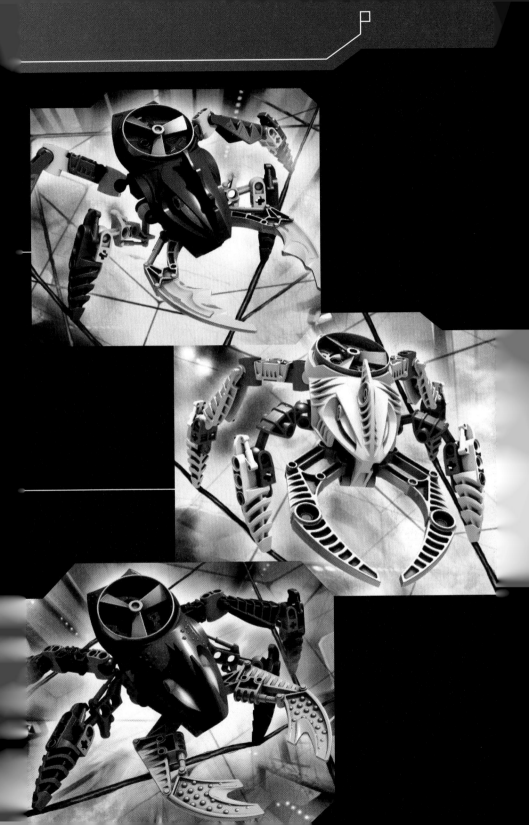

DOMAIN: ZONE OF DARKNESS

The Zivon is a massive Rahi, well over 30 feet tall, that first appeared in Metru Nui after the coming of the Visorak hordes. Its natural domain is the Zone of Darkness about which very little is known other than that it can apparently be accessed by the spinners of Kahgarak.

This monstrosity's head resembles that of a Visorak, but its claws are crablike and its stinger similar to that of a Nui-Jaga. When fighting something of its own size, it will seize the enemy in its claws and then sting repeatedly. Its hard shell protects it from most damage. The Zivon is also capable of shooting webbing from its legs to entangle a foe.

Despite the fact that the Zivon fights alongside the Visorak, the spider creatures hate and fear it. It's well known that the Zivon only aids them as a way of protecting its food source, since it eats Visorak. A Zivon's "victory celebration" often involves consuming half of its allies. The only known specimen of this creature was last seen being transported back into the field of darkness, locked in combat with the Tahtorak.

Rahaga Norik says: "If there is a way to stop a Zivon, I don't know it. It can be thrown the length of a metru, have a building dropped on it, be slammed head first into the ground, and come right back at you again. Smoke and flame can sometimes slow it down, but not defeat it. At best, you can hope it will be trapped in the Zone of Darkness again if a Kahgarak chooses to send it there. Otherwise, the appearance of a Zivon is a good sign that it is time to move elsewhere."

There are dozens of species of Rahi, and not every one could fit into this book. Here is a quick look at some of the other creatures of Metru Nui:

ARCHIVES BEAST:

A strange creature housed in the Onu-Metru Archives and believed to have some connection to the *reconstitutes at random* Kanoka disk power. It was evidently able to take on any shape it wished, once appearing as an empty room.

ASH BEAR:

An ursine creature known for its sharp teeth and claws. A few specimens were at large in the mountains of Po-Metru prior to the Great Cataclysm, with most in the Archives. All are now free.

BOG SNAKE:

Nasty, venomous serpents who live in the muddy shallows off Onu-Metru and feed on small amphibians.

BRAKAS:

Mischievous monkeylike creatures who once roamed freely through Le-Metru and Ga-Metru. They were such pests that the Matoran petitioned Turaga Dume to have them banned. Vahki later rounded up all specimens and put them in the Archives, from which they have since escaped.

CAVE FISH:

A Ga-Matoran creature that defends itself by absorbing liquid protodermis through its skin and using the fluid to "inflate" itself and give the appearance of a larger creature.

DIKAPI:

A flightless desert bird known for its great endurance.

FIKOU:

Tree spiders known for nesting in Le-Metru cables. Considered to be highly dangerous.

FIREFLYER:

Flying insects with a fiery sting. Swarms of fireflyers have been known to nest in furnaces and maintenance tunnels beneath Ta-Metru.

FUSA:

A kangaroo-like Rahi and a natural enemy of the Muaka. Fusa defend themselves using their powerful hind legs.

GHEKULA:

Amphibious creatures most often found in swampy waters. It is considered bad luck to harm one.

HAPAKA:

Large hounds briefly employed by Ga-Matoran to drive away Kavinika, with mixed success.

HIKAKI:

A small lizardlike creature that thrives on molten protodermis and often shares territory with the Furnace Salamander.

HOTO:

Fire bugs known for tunneling through buildings, using the searing heat given off by their bodies to melt the way.

HUSI:

An ostrichlike bird that once roamed free on the rocky crags of Po-Metru, before being hunted almost to extinction by Muaka and other predators. They were later placed in the Archives for their own protection.

ICE BAT:

Winged creatures known for their destructive flights through Ko-Metru Knowledge Towers. Ice Bats are the favored prey of crystal climbers.

INFERNAVIKA:

A small bird that makes its home near the molten protodermis waste pipes on the coast of Ta-Metru. Its love of ultra-hot places keeps it safe, as few other creatures venture near.

KERAS:

Large coral crabs found in the ocean off Ga-Metru.

KIRIKORI NUI:

Locustlike insects known for their appearances in the skies over Metru Nui every ten years or so. They would alight in Po-Metru and Ga-Metru, consume all the vegetation in sight, and then disappear. Their point of origin is unknown.

KOFO-JAGA:

Small, fiery scorpions known for attacking in swarms, these are most often found in abandoned forges in Ta-Metru. They are attracted to the smell of molten protodermis and prefer dark places. Ta-Matoran investigating empty factories know to carry bright lightstones to protect themselves (temporarily) from these creatures.

KUMA-NUI:

A giant rat creature found in the maintenance tunnels beneath the Archives, particularly in the Ta-Metru and Ko-Metru areas.

LAVA EEL:

A serpentlike creature of Ta-Metru, occasionally kept as pets by Ta-Matoran. When agitated, the surface temperature of a lava eel's skin increases to the point where it can melt through metal.

LIGHTFISH:

Small, glowing fish found in the deepest underwater caves around Ga-Metru.

MAHIKA:

A large and dangerous cave toad found in Ga-Metru. It has few natural predators since it is poisonous to most other Rahi.

MAKUTA FISH:

An incredibly ugly breed of fish capable of leaping from the water to attack larger creatures.

MATA NUI FISHING BIRD:

Clever and noisy birds often seen splashing along the Le-Metru coastline. Too fast for most aquatic predators, these birds seem to delight in teasing their enemies by gliding close to them, then soaring away at the last moment.

NIGHT CREEPER:

A nocturnal creature found in Onu-Metru. Roughly seven feet long, squat, with powerful legs, night creepers forage for small insects and rodents.

NUI-KOPEN:

A giant wasplike insect and a bitter enemy of the Nui-Rama, since both hunt the same prey.

POKAWI:

A flightless fowl that lives high among the peaks of Po-Metru, feeding on whatever vegetation that might be there. Their high vantage point is all that saves them, since they can usually spot predators long before they get too close.

PROTODITES:

Microscopic creatures accidentally freed in the Archives and now infesting some sections. The preferred prey of Archives Moles.

RAHI NUI:

A monstrous hybrid creature, with the head of a Kane-Ra Bull, the forearms of a Tarakava, the body and hind legs of a Muaka, the wings of a Nui-Rama, and the tail stinger of a Nui-Jaga. When first encountered by the Toa Metru, the Rahi Nui also possessed the six basic Kanoka disk powers. It was responsible for severely wounding Toa Nokama before finally being defeated.

RANAMA:

A giant fire frog that often makes a home in the molten protodermis that runs through Ta-Metru. Ranama feed on small insects, leaping out of the vats to snare them with its tongue. They are hated by Ta-Matoran, both for the fact that they must be filtered from the protodermis and for their habit of attacking anything that comes too close.

RAZORFISH:

Misnamed, this is actually an aquatic mammal whose body is lined with incredibly sharp scales. Merely brushing against it is enough to cause serious wounds. Razorfish have been known to accidentally make huge gashes in the sides of passing Matoran boats.

ROCK LION:

A mysterious creature said to inhabit the lowest levels of the Archives. Its teeth and claws are extremely sharp and the tendrils of its mane become white-hot when the creature is angered.

RUKI:

Small fish commonly found in the ocean around Metru Nui. Though not physically imposing, they do have extremely powerful jaws and schools of them have been known to drive off Tarakava.

SAND TARAKAVA:

A slightly smaller cousin of the amphibious Tarakava, this creature dwells in the sandy wastes of Po-Metru. It hides beneath the sand, waiting for prey to pass near. The sand Tarakava is a mortal enemy of the Kikanalo.

TAKEA SHARK:

The "king of sharks" and a fierce enemy of the Tarakava. A constant menace to Matoran vessels, which it attacks seemingly for sport.

TAKU:

A ducklike bird believed to be related to the Gukko. It is known for its ability to dive deep beneath the water to find fish.

TARAKAVA NUI:

An extremely large version of a Tarakava, possibly a mutation. Its origin is unknown.

TUNNELER:

A reptilian creature of Po-Metru capable of taking on the properties of any physical object used against it (a fireball, for example, turns it into a creature of fire).

VATUKA:

A legendary creature made of rock. No one is quite sure if it should be considered a Rahi or something more sinister, just as no Matoran can say for certain that such a creature even exists.

WAIKIRU:

A walruslike creature that dwells on the shore of Ga-Metru. Swift and agile in the water, they are clumsy on land. They rely on their tusks to drive away predators, primarily Takea Sharks.